LUCY FLINT

My Girlfriend's Friends

First edition

This book was professionally typeset on Reedsy.
Find out more at reedsy.com

Contents

1

Another Flavor

A few years ago, when I was in university I dated this girl, let's call her Lola, who was one of those "girl squads". Lola is 22, 5,6ft and cute as hell, blonde hair, blue eyes, always tanned from being outside. She's sporty and despite being petite, she had these bouncy C-cup tits that fit almost perfectly in my hands. Her ass was firm and toned and although she did a lot of squats it wasn't big at all, which I prefer anyway.

Lola and her 3 best friends were the kinds of friends that call each other their soulmates. I know, pretty cliché but whatever. They were close, seeing each other almost every day, talking all the time, telling each other everything kind of close. Three of the four had known each other since middle school and the other girl they'd met in college and become close with immediately.

Anyway, so when Lola and I first began dating she told me that her "squad" would always come first in her life. I rolled my eyes a little and shrugged it off, honestly, I wasn't looking for anything serious with her anyway. But I ended up dating this girl for longer than I expected. We got on well and the sex was great but mainly I think that most of the drama I had to deal with other girls I'd dated didn't exist here because Lola talked about that stuff with her friends and not me. I knew she talked about our sex life in detail to her friends, which to be honest kind of turned me on because they were a sexy bunch. Now might be a good time to describe her friends, Miley, Ekin-Su, and Jennifer.

Miley is a short skinny easy-going Asian girl with straight black hair and a great smile. She's probably the one I'm least attracted to but whose personality I liked best. She and I usually made eye contact when one of the other girls said something dumb.

Ekin-Su is around medium height, pale-skinned, and has platinum-shock blonde hair. She looks like the kind of girl who spends hours in front of the mirror every day, always with perfect make-up, perfect nails, etc. Her body is hot overall, but what stands out is her bubble butt, which she shows off at every opportunity. She usually wore those booty shorts where half her ass would hang out and then she would point out every guy that stared at her. I'm not an ass man but it certainly was an eye-catcher. Ekin-Su is also the newest addition to the group, the others have known her for only two or so years at this point.

Now each of them was a smoke show in their own way but Jennifer is probably one of the hottest girls I'd ever seen in real life. Seriously this girl belonged on a runway somewhere. She had light brown skin, shiny dark brown hair to her waist, and hourglass proportions. Her tits were incredible, natural double Ds at least and they looked unbelievable on her shapely body. She often wore outfits that showcased her rack, and she had a 10/10 face to match her body. She wore dark red lipstick a lot and did this thing sometimes where she would bite her lip while making eye contact with you and that's how I discovered a new kink I didn't know I had. When I saw her for the first time I thought "Shit I picked the wrong friend", which I know is kind of shitty, but I couldn't help it.

Unfortunately, it turned out she had this bitchy personality, and I couldn't talk to her for more than 5 mins at a time without getting annoyed. Still, I couldn't help but stare at her sometimes which I think Lola noticed.

About a month into dating Lola, we were chilling on the couch in her apartment, watching some random show on Netflix. Lola began absentmindedly rubbing her fingers on my dick over my shorts. I had closed my eyes and was enjoying the feeling when she suddenly said, "doesn't that actress look like Jennifer?" I opened my eyes to see two actors making out. The actress was hot and had long brown hair but apart from that, she didn't look like Jennifer at all. Honestly, Jennifer was way hotter. "I guess," I said and closed my eyes again. Lola took my dick out of my shorts and began stroking it, "Seriously look at her, don't you think she's hot?"

I was confused at this point and looked at the screen again. The actress was topless now and they were clearly about to have sex. Lola was stroking my dick now and she looked horny. Without thinking I said, "Jennifer has bigger tits". For a second after I said that I thought fuck I'm in for it. But Lola just smiled at me knowingly and began stroking faster. At this point, I was hard as a rock and confused as hell but also, I didn't care. For some reason, this was turning Lola on. I'd take it.

I leaned forward to kiss her and reached under her loose t-shirt to grab her tits. She yanked her shirt off revealing her cute bouncy boobs. She had bikini tan lines from spending time on the beach so most of her skin was golden-brown, but her boobs were pale. Her nipples were pink larger than you'd expect on her tits which I always found sexy. I reached out to grab one hard

3

nipple, but Lola pulled away from me, getting her phone out. Wtf? She was still jerking me with one hand, but she seemed to be scrolling through Insta gram with the other.

"Lola, what's going on?" She handed me her phone and on it was a picture of Jennifer on the beach. She was standing with her back to the camera but with the top half of her body twisted around to look at the camera. She was wearing a nonexistent G-string that had disappeared into her beautiful ass and !!!! she was topless with her hands covering her nipples. She was laughing and looking straight at the camera, with her boobs spilling over on either side of her hands. Holy. Shit. I needed to join Insta. I don't know what my expression was as I looked at this photo but when I looked up Lola had the most wicked smile on her face.

She leaned forward to kiss me and then knelt in front of the couch and took my dick in her mouth as she had done so many times before. Except for this time, I was holding a photo of her nearly naked friend as she sucked my dick. Although a part of my brain was wondering if this was a test, most of my brain was focusing on trying to memorize the scene in front of me. I couldn't keep my eyes off Jennifer's pic.

My eyes zoomed in on her magnificent tits and I tried imagining the nipples her hands were hiding. I reached down and grabbed Lola's tits, massaging them, and thinking about Jennifer's body. I felt her nipples stiffen and I pulled on them till she gasped. Lola was licking up and down my dick, pausing to suck on the tip.

Usually, she makes eye contact while doing this but today her eyes were closed. Because she wanted me to look at the picture?? I imagined Jennifer in the same position, her beautiful mouth worshipping my cock. My dick began to throb. Lola was sucking

4

on the tip like a lollipop while stroking me with both her hands. In between sucking she looked up and me and said, "would you fuck her?"

Holy shit. Did she want a threesome? Fuck. I was too dazed to say anything other than "yeah," but I was thinking God exists and loves me.

"What would you do to her?" Lola was saying

"Oh fuck. I'd fuck her brains out". I know, I'm not Shakespeare but it was the best I could do.

"What else?" She began deepthroating my cock.

I groaned as her lips touched my body and put my hands on her head to hold her there. "I'd fuck her mouth like this," I said and began to thrust into Lola's throat. I felt her gag, but she pushed her head down to keep her lips on my body. I've never known a girl who could suck dick like her.

My filthy fantasies were flowing out of me in paragraphs now. "I'd hold her beautiful face like this and make her worship my cock. Then I'd fuck her wet pussy until she begs me to stop." With each sentence, I was thrusting into Lola's throat and could feel myself beginning to cum. I closed my eyes and imagined it was Jennifer moaning under me, her tits bouncing as I slid in and out of her pussy.

I couldn't believe what I was saying but I kept going, "I wanna cum all over her huge tits, and then I'll make you lick my cum off her body." Lola struggled a little, gagging as my cum shot into her throat. I held her head in place for a moment and I thrust into her throat one last time. I released her so that my dick left her throat but stayed in her mouth. I continued moving her head up and down my dick, staring into her eyes as I came in her beautiful mouth.

When I finished coming, I released her head, and she showed

me my cum in her mouth and waited for me to nod before swallowing it.

I pulled her up onto the couch and kissed her deeply, shoving my hand into her panties. My fingers slipped between her legs, to find that she was unbelievably wet. I realized she had been touching herself I as throat-fucked her and described my fantasies about one of her best friends. She gasped as I began rubbing circles on her clit. "What. The. Fuck. Was. That?" I asked her. She struggled a little, but I held her firmly and continued rubbing her clit. "What's going on Lola?" She moaned, "I- we have a rule."

"A rule?"

"A rule that whenever one of us has a steady boyfriend. The others get to fuck him once."

"What?!" I could feel my dick starting to get hard again even though I'd just come. I slipped a finger into Lola's pussy and continued rubbing her clit with my thumb. She began to shudder and moan. I stopped fingering her.

"No, no, please!"

"Then keep talking," I said, slowly fucking her pussy with two fingers.

"It's, so no one gets jealous. Before the rule. There were incidents, fights". I took one round pink nipple in my mouth and sucked on it hard. She nearly screamed, "no cheating, no jealousy. It works well...one time...."

She was barely coherent, but I got the gist of it. I was going to get to fuck all three of her best friends. I continued sucking on her tit as I finger-banged her and stimulated her clit. Lola came suddenly, screaming and moaning and thrashing under me. We lay silently on the couch, both panting for what felt like ages. Eventually, she turned her head to look at me. "So," she said, a smile spreading across her face, "who do you want first?"

My girlfriend Lola and I were lying on our couch. Shortly before, she'd told me that she and her friends have a rule where if one of them has a steady boyfriend, the others all get to fuck him one time, for friendship reasons. I was staring at Lola open-mouthed. I couldn't believe what I was hearing, it was like I'd slipped into some kind of porno version of my life - except it was happening. Part of me, specifically the lower part of me, was thinking that I must be the luckiest guy in the world. But I also couldn't shake the feeling that Lola was playing some kind of joke on me. She looked like she was enjoying my confusion as she waited for me to answer her. But I had some questions first.

"How did this happen?" was the first one. Over the course of the next half hour, Lola told me about all the girl-crew drama that had led to this rule. I'd picked up on some of it from things that were said in passing and some previous conversations from when we first started dating, but I have to admit that I'd never paid close attention until then. But now it was all vitally important. It helped that now every time she mentioned one of her friends, I'd wonder what they looked like naked, what they would sound like in bed. Anyway, I digress.

The short version is that Miley's high school boyfriend had cheated on her with Jennifer (which Jennifer confessed to her out of guilt), and Miley had slept with one of Jennifer's exes for revenge. Later, Lola and Jennifer competed over the same guy and things got ugly. These incidents had caused so much jealousy and anger that they'd all nearly stopped being friends. They decided that no guy would come before their friendship and came up with this rule for when they arrived at college. They met Ekin-Su when it turned out that her boyfriend was hitting on and trying to hook up with multiple girls in the squad. Ekin-Su dumped the guy and ended up joining the squad.

The rule worked well because it dispensed of the need for competitiveness and instead made them all feel excited and slutty when any of them dated someone new. Lola said it had made them more open and honest with each other, bringing them closer than ever. She also said that the offer wasn't presented right away and not to every guy but only after he'd been around for a while and the girls had talked it over first. I realized this meant that not only had Lola already been planning this with the other girls but that they had all decided they wanted to fuck me, wow!

To be honest, I didn't quite get how the rule and all of it worked but I wasn't about to poke holes. I was now convinced that this wasn't some elaborate joke, and I was going to get to sleep with all of them, so I wasn't trying to shoot myself in the foot. I took a minute to fervently applaud my past self for asking Lola out on a date rather than just letting it remain a casual hook-up as I initially intended. I had a few more pressing questions; however, would Lola have to sleep with someone else if one of the girls got a new boyfriend?

"No", she said, "it's only the girls who are single at the time. And obviously, no one must do anything they don't want to! It's not like there's a contract. It's just a way for us to prove to each other that our friendship comes first." Next question, had it happened already? "Yes, twice," Lola said, laughing at my expression. Her breasts bounced slightly as she laughed, distracting me, and making my cock harden again. She explained that while there had been other guys who had gotten to fuck one or two of the squad, because the others were either not single or not interested, only two lucky guys had had the chance to fuck all four of these gorgeous girls. And I was going

8

to be lucky bastard number 3. My dick was hard again. Lola felt it press against her stomach and laughed, grabbing it in her hands.

"You're not jealous?" I asked her. She licked her fingers and rubbed her spit on my dickhead, looking down as she answered, "no, in fact, it turns me on, a lot!"

My dick felt rock-hard now. I put a hand under her chin and tilted her face up, so she was looking at me. "You know that I'm. submissive" she said, looking into my eyes, "the last two guys, well, they weren't my guys, but now with you. the truth is I love the idea of being with an alpha man, who could have any girl he wanted, whose cock has been inside all of my friends."

Holy fuck. Guys let me tell you, I work out but I'm far from the strongest guy I know. I'm pretty decent looking but I wouldn't win any awards. But at that moment, I felt like goddamn superman. Just think of the biggest Chad in the world- at that moment, I was him. Without a word, I flipped Lola onto her back and grabbed her legs with my hands, spreading them and pushing them back onto her. Lola gasped and locked her elbows around her knees, so she was clutching her legs against her chest.

I was kneeling in front of her, with her legs spread before me and her beautiful pink pussy exposed. I froze with my dick in my hand, picturing one by one each of her friends in the same position, their legs spread, pussies ready. I thrust my cock into her sopping wet pussy in one motion and began fucking her like a mad man. Lola was screaming and hugging her legs to her chest as her tits bounced.

She had told me before that she liked rough dominant sex and kinky slightly degrading dirty talk. We'd experimented with it a little, but I'd never fully gotten into the zone. But now, watching her writhing and moaning under me, it seemed to come more naturally. With a great effort, I pulled out of her and placed my cock on top of her pussy. Her eyes shot open, "no- no, come back!"

"No," I said simply, ignoring my throbbing cock. She made to unlock her arms, but I grabbed her knees and held them spread apart, trapping her arms. I was enjoying the view too much to let it go.

"Did I tell you could move? Keep your legs open".

Lola nodded; panting "okay".

"Okay?" I asked, raising my eyebrows as I stroked my cock against her clit. She shivered like I'd sent a shock through her body.

"I mean yes, baby..., of course"

I held my dick with one hand, with the other one on her thigh, making sure her legs stayed spread. I brought my dick to her wet entrance and dipped it in, before pulling out again. "Oh yes, yes, no," she was moaning. Her moans were getting me going but I tried to stay focused. I brought my dick back up and stroked her clit with it, going faster and faster until she trembled and moaned, "fuck me fuck me please."

"Please what?" I demanded.

She looked at me trying to figure out what I wanted. I could see that she would say anything that would get my cock back in her, but I wasn't about to give it to her until I got the right answer.

"Please." she tried again. I shook my head.

Lola stared at me for a moment and then pressed her knees firmly into her chest, and lifted her ass slightly, presenting both her holes to me. She pulled her legs apart as far as they would go so that her pussy lips spread open by themselves. Then she

looked me right in the eyes and in a soft low voice said, "please...,
sir, fuck my pussy, sir, I need it."

I groaned. Fuck, that'd do. I brought my cock back to
her entrance and thrust forward, letting her warm wet pussy
envelop me. I slammed into her, with my eyes closed and held
her firmly as I thrust in and out. She tried to prompt me to keep
talking dirty to her, but I ignored her, using her hole only for my
pleasure. I continued fucking her letting her tight pussy drain
my cock fully before pulling out. Lola had been screaming and
moaning this whole time.

When I pulled out, she finally relaxed and flipped on her side
immediately, panting and gasping. I slid my hand between her
legs to feel her drenched pussy, which was now leaking cum. I
looked up to see Lola smiling at me. It was amazing how quickly
she transformed from a desperate sub to a confident tease. She
was still breathing heavily as she looked at me and said, "so are
you going to answer MY question now? Who do you want first?"

If you've read the chapters so far you know that my heart,
brain, and boner were thumping to the uneven beat of And-rea,
And-rea, And-rea, the smoking hot brunette with the unreal
body. So why didn't I just come out and say it? I'm not sure. I
mean Lola surely knew. Not too long ago she'd watched me blow
my load into her mouth while gaping at a photo of Jennifer. I
just wanted to play it cool, the post-nut clarity was telling me
not to make it obvious just how pronounced my preference for
her best friend's body was.

Instead, I kissed Lola and said something like, "I don't know,
I need some time to process". Lola laughed, "not too long, it'd
be cruel to make them wait for a cock this good". I think I was
falling in love with this girl.

My girlfriend Lola had just told me that she had, what I would later learn is called, a "cuckquean's fetish", meaning she got off on the thought of me with other girls. So, thanks to the rule between her and her friends I would not only fuck her 3 best friends, but it was also going to make things hotter in bed between my girlfriend and me. I'd won the damn lottery.

The rest of the week was crazy. In between classes, I was spending every spare moment at the gym. I'm already pretty fit but considering the situation, you can't blame me for trying to get in the best shape possible. I would occasionally see one of the other girls, Jennifer, Miley, and Ekin-Su, on campus, and we'd wave to each other. I'm sure I wasn't imagining their blushes and smirks, but no one stopped to chat.

Nevertheless, my imagination would run wild, and I'd end up rushing to Lola's and bending her over her desk. Ever since our talk, our sex life had been off the charts. We were fucking multiple times a day now and practically living together. It was very a free-use situation at this point because all I had to do was think about the amazing experiences in store for me and I'd get a rock-hard boner and need to use Lola's mouth or pussy to take care of it. This resulted in me often texting her on the way to her place to wait for me with her legs spread or her mouth open.

Lola was loving these developments as we'd also been experimenting more with her cuckquean's fetish. Something that we started doing during this time that we both enjoyed was Lola sucking my cock blindfolded while I watched Point of View porn. The sounds from the porn combined with how vulnerable she felt drove her crazy. I have some hot memories from this period, which I can write about some other time. But you're here now for another saga.

Lola had spoken to her friends, and they were planning on going clubbing together that weekend. I was invited to come along and see how things went. Everyone involved knew what this meant, I would go home with one of the other girls that day. I'm not going to pretend I hadn't considered what you're thinking, orgy! But I thought, firstly if that were an option Lola would have mentioned it. I didn't want to do or say anything to jeopardize my current situation. Secondly, although the thought of Jennifer and Ekin-Su making out with my cock between their lips was a scene I'd imagined many times.

Realistically in a 5-person orgy, I wouldn't be able to give each girl the full attention I would want to give them. Exploring these girls one by one and fucking each of them as they deserved was better than one crazy night. The fact that I would get to go dancing with them and choose the babe I wanted first was the cherry on the cake.

Even though many of Jennifer's Instagram posts now sat in a special folder on my phone, I still was not sure which girl I wanted first. The conflict in my mind went something like this, on one hand, I'd had the hots for Jennifer since the day I met her and if I could have her, I didn't want to wait another minute.

On the other hand, I thought her pussy might ruin me. don't laugh, I mean it. I'm not a masochist it's just that each of these girls was a babe and this was a once-in-a-lifetime opportunity. I was sure that once I fucked Jennifer, I wouldn't be able to get her out of my head for a while. Wouldn't it be better to save the best for last? I wanted to cherish each step on my stairway to heaven and Jennifer rightfully belonged at the top.

This is what I was telling myself when the weekend finally arrived. I was going to take either Ekin-Su or Miley home and fuck her brains out. Lola and I were stupid horny the day leading up to the clubbing. I'd woken up to the sound of her moaning and fingering herself in bed next to me, which incidentally is far better than an alarm clock.

That night she put on a blue sequin mini dress and high heels that she looked stunning in. After so much instant gratification it was hard not to force her onto her knees right then and there, but I had a long night ahead of me. We had a few drinks, but I was careful not to drink too much and we were all over each other on the way to the club. Lola genuinely seemed as excited as I was, which was a total turn-on.

We got to the club sometime after midnight. Try and remember what a packed club in a college town looked like on Saturday in pre-pandemic times. Miley was waiting for us in line. She and Lola squealed and hugged and kissed like they hadn't seen each other just two days ago. Normally I would hug her too, but I didn't know what the protocol was. How do you greet your girlfriend's friend that you or may not be fucking that night? Miley reached up to hug me and said, "Su and Jennifer are inside already". She looked at me meaningfully, smirking, and then looked me up and down in an obvious way, "not bad". "Not bad yourself," I said automatically, but then I checked her out. Lola was texting on her phone and seemed distracted.

Miley was wearing a black tube top that ended inches above her pierced navel. The outline of her small tits was easily visible, and I wondered if she was wearing anything underneath the top. Below she wore a short skirt that flared out, like a schoolgirl skirt. Her straight black hair fell to her shoulders and her cute Chinese features weren't covered in much make-up. She was so short and skinny that although she was wearing high heels, she had to go up on her toes to hug me. I've said before that she was not my type but there was no internal debate, she looked hot. I hadn't noticed her navel piercing before and it was stirring something inside me. By the time all this was over, how many more new kinks would I discover? She noticed me checking her out and grinned.

Eventually, we got inside, and Lola and Miley rushed off to get us shots. I elbowed my way through the crowd, looking for the other girls. When I saw them, my heart nearly stopped. Ekin-Su and Jennifer were dancing together, and I swear every guy within a 20 feet radius was staring at them. Ekin-Su as always had half her ass on display. She was wearing one of those tight skirts that looks like they had been ripped apart and then stitched back together. It looked something like this. She looked, there was no other way to describe it, trashy, but in a way that no guy would ever complain about. She was sticking her ass out as she danced, so much that the stitches on her skirt seemed about to snap, which I don't know if she would have had a problem with.

I was getting pretty turned on watching her slutty display, but then she moved out of the way, and I properly saw Jennifer. All other thoughts left my brain. She was smiling and laughing as she danced, looking around at the many guys staring at her with open mouths. I was one of those guys. Jennifer was wearing an incredible red dress which was practically slashed down the middle in the front. Her long dark brown hair was tied up in a high ponytail, allowing for a clear view of her magnificent breasts. I'm not even going to try to describe them because there are no words. At that moment I forgot about all my plans, the stairway to heaven, and all that nonsense, the only thought in my mind was having her. Right away. I went up to her and put my hands on her waist. Both she and Su immediately started squealing and hugging me and asking where the other girls were. I wrapped one arm around Jennifer's waist and pointed with the other hand to the bar where I could see Lola and Miley over the crowd.

Su looked confused for half a second and then zoned in on my arm around Jennifer's waist. She giggled and shrugged, "okay I'll go join them at the bar".

As soon as she left, I spun Jennifer, so she was facing me. Her gorgeous face was just inches away from mine and I could feel her hot breath on my face. My hands were on her waist, stroking her lightly as we moved to the music. She looked into my eyes and smirked, "impatient, aren't you?" I didn't know what else to say but "that dress, you're stunning. You're the most beautiful girl here tonight."

I don't know if that was wrong to say, since Lola was there too but it was true.

Jennifer simply said, "I know".

I wanted to kiss that stupid overconfident smirk off her face, but it felt too intimate. Instead, I let my hands wander lower, so I was gripping her perfect ass. I pulled her against me, so her breasts were pressed against my chest. Only a few layers of clothing between us. I rubbed her butt, and her breath quickened, one hand slipped through the slit on the side of her dress to touch underneath the fabric. I groaned audibly when I felt her ass, she was either wearing a G-string thong or no panties, I couldn't feel any fabric. My dick had sprung to attention, and I was grateful for the crowded and dark dancefloor. Jennifer felt my cock pressing up against her and she gasped "Liam!" I spun her around, so her ass was lined up with my dick. I began to grind softly into her ass, still gripping her waist.

The club lights were flashing and in odd moments I could see the jealous looks of guys who had been watching her, wondering how I'd scored a girl like her. Jennifer was softly rubbing her ass against my hard dick as she moved in time to the music. I brushed her hair out of the way, and she leaned to one side, extending her neck before me. I leaned forward to kiss her neck and she let out a soft moan when my lips touched her skin. We stayed like this in my heaven for a few moments, with me kissing up and down Jennifer's neck, breathing in her scent and her letting out these soft sexy moans while she rubbed her ass on me. My hands had just begun to travel up the curves of her body towards her tits when she suddenly froze.

She put her hands over my palms and tried to step away.

"What's up?" I said in her ear, shouting over the music. "I'm sorry Liam, I can't!" What was wrong? She turned to face me, and I leaned down to hear her. Ironically, I had a perfect view of her tits as she explained that she'd met this guy not long ago and they'd been on a few dates. She was telling me that she liked him, and she wanted to see where things would go with him, so she couldn't "do anything" with me. Wtf?? I asked the obvious question, why hadn't Lola known about this? They usually told each other everything immediately, Lola got calls in the middle of the night sometimes. Jennifer shrugged, "I hadn't gotten around to it yet," she said smirking at me and biting her lip. That didn't make sense, it also didn't answer the other obvious question, if she didn't want to "do anything" why had she teased me with her ass and let me make out with her neck?

I looked at the way she was smirking at me and realized that she hadn't told the other girls for the same reason that she'd just been grinding on my dick – she was playing with me. She had wanted to see if I would choose her first, and how badly I wanted her. She knew how attracted I was to her; I was sure Lola had told her about the Instagram incident. And she deliberately hadn't said anything to Lola so that she could lead me on and then turn me down. Fuck. I'd forgotten what a bitch she was. I hope I don't sound like an incel! It wasn't simply that she didn't want me but that she'd purposely tried to humiliate me for her amusement.

Jennifer was watching me work all this out and smiling at me, still holding my palms in hers. I released her hands and turned away. I don't know what I would have said next but luckily the other girls got there just then. Well, just Su and Miley. I took the tequila shots Miley was holding out to me and tossed them down my throat immediately. I felt like I'd just been hit in the face, or maybe more like kicked in the balls. I was sure my face was red, and Miley was looking at me with concern. Jennifer and Su were whispering to each other, but I didn't care. "Where's Lola?" I asked Miley.

"Um, Lola left", Miley told me, looking confused. "She uh. saw. you and Jennifer and. I think she wanted to give you privacy..."

"Oh, that's just great."

"Are you okay?"

"I need some air." I wanted to be alone. I turned around and pushed through the crowd, heading for the exit. I already had a cigarette lit by the time I realized that Miley had followed me outside.

"What the hell happened?"

I explained as briefly as possible, in short, clipped sentences. Outside of the chaos of the club, I felt irritated but no longer as humiliated as before. Miley exhaled in a whistle, "that bitch". I laughed and shrugged trying to act like I didn't care. Miley was pulling something out of her purse. She held a spliff up and grinned at me, "forget her. Let's have some fun. You up for it?"

I nodded. We passed the spliff back and forth just chatting and shooting the shit. My head was soon spinning from the combination of the booze and the weed, but I still felt better than I had some minutes ago. Miley was just so easy to talk to. There was one drag left on the spliff when she said, "come here I want to try something".

She yanked me down, so I was face-to-face with her and then took the final drag of the spliff. She put her tiny hands on either side of our mouths, blocking the air out and then blew the smoke from her mouth directly into my mouth. Her hot drunken breath was so much more intoxicating than the weed that I did what came naturally and kissed her.

I don't know how long we made out but when we came up for air, we were both breathing heavily. Without any discussion, we headed straight to her place. No sooner had Miley's door closed behind us than I was all over her. I pushed her against the wall and slid my hand underneath her tube top, confirming my suspicions that she was not wearing anything beneath it. My hands explored her small, pointed tits as I helped Miley wriggle out of her top.

Her barely-there tits were not something I'd usually be into but at that moment the unfamiliarity of her body was especially sexy. I reached out and took a nipple each between my forefinger and thumb, rubbing them slowly till Miley began moaning and shivering in response. My dick was straining against my jeans, I couldn't believe I was actually in Miley's apartment, undressing her and making her moan. With one hand I went up her skirt, coming to a wet spot in her panties. Miley gasped and stood with her legs a little further apart. Fuck. Especially after everything that had happened that night, seeing how much she wanted me was a real turn-on. I didn't bother with taking her skirt off, I simply pushed her panties to the side and slid two fingers inside her tight pussy.

She let out this small shriek and trembled as I started to fuck

19

her with my fingers. To her credit, she was trying very hard to focus on getting my clothes off. She'd successfully gotten my shirt off and was fumbling with the button on my jeans. Soon she had my throbbing cock out. Her tiny hands making my cock look huge was another advantage to fucking a petite chick that I couldn't have predicted. She began stroking my dick, but I couldn't take any more stimulation, I had to get inside her. I took my fingers out of her and pushed her up against the wall again, lifting her by the waist. She immediately wrapped her legs around me and leaned into me.

I pulled her panties aside and lined my cock up against her dripping pussy. With her wet panties still on, I pressed my cock into her warm hole. Her pussy was so incredibly tight around my dick that I felt like I could barely move inside her but after a few thrusts, I could feel her adjusting to my cock. Miley was moaning in my ear as I began to really fuck her.

"Right there" she kept saying, "yeah right there". I'd love to tell you that I fucked her all night like a porn star but the alcohol, the novelty of a new pussy, and the incredible position of fucking while carrying a girl, which I had never done before, combined meant that I wouldn't be lasting very long.

Soon enough I was shooting hot cum into Miley's pussy, thinking too late that I should've probably used a condom. I was honestly too far gone to care at that moment. When I was done, I lifted her off my dick and watched with satisfaction as my come dripped down her legs. Her bed was just a few feet away, but we hadn't made it there. I carried her there and dropped her unceremoniously on the bed. Miley didn't seem to mind. She looked exhausted and sweaty, but she was smiling. "You never even took all my clothes off," she said. "Sorry," I said, although I wasn't really. But Miley was taking her skirt off already, and then her panties. She lay back on the bed and spread her legs, giving me a perfect view of her tiny creampied Asian pussy. Rubbing Miley's clit while watching me cum slowly leak out of her is another image I'll never forget for as long as I live. After she came, there was a lot of kissing and cuddling and although I hadn't intended to, I fell asleep next to her. I woke up a few hours later and looked at my phone to check the time.

On my lock screen were several messages from Lola:

"You looked like you were going to fuck Jennifer right there in the club"

"I want to taste her pussy on your cock"

"Can't wait to hear all about it"#

Miley had long been my favorite of Lola's girl squad. She was the only one of my girlfriend's friends that I'd been able to see as my friend as well. Then last night I'd pushed her skinny Asian body up against a wall and fucked her with her wet panties on and left me cum deep inside her pussy. It was safe to say that I wouldn't see her as just a buddy anymore. All things considered; I was completely fine with that.

I had just woken up in Miley's bed after accidentally falling asleep there. My girlfriend Lola had been sending me horny text messages for half the night which I was reading on my lock screen.

"You looked like you were going to fuck Jennifer right there in the club"

"I want to taste her pussy on your cock"

"Can't wait to hear all about it"

Clearly, she'd been getting off to the thought of me fucking Jennifer. Although that hadn't happened, the idea of my girl-friend sitting at home thinking of me while I spent the night fucking one of her best friends...wow.

I unlocked my phone and opened Lola's chat to answer her. I had expected that the three texts I'd seen were only the last of a long series of messages. What I hadn't expected to see among the texts was this image over a text that said, "waiting for you at your place". Holy shit. Even while I lay in bed next to a different naked girl, Lola knew how to get my attention. Attractive as the thought of round 2 with Miley was, I owed the girl who was making this all happen. On the other hand, I didn't want to sneak out of Miley's place like a thief in the night, she deserved better.

I gently disentangled myself and moved to the foot of the bed. Miley was sleeping on her back with one leg up to the side, giving me a nice view of her tiny Asian pussy. I reached out to spread her pussy lips with my fingers and bent forward to taste her clit. I heard Miley gasp and felt her move but I didn't look up. I began to move my tongue in circles at the same time I heard her start moaning.

She spread her legs wider apart and slightly raised her hips. She began moving like that like she was gently humping my face. Fuck. This girl was full of surprises. Each time she moved upwards; my tongue was flattened against her wet pussy. I was tasting not just her clit but getting her pussy juices all over my mouth. I moved my tongue around, tasting her inner lips and very lightly sucking on her clit.

Miley's legs snapped shut around my head and she moaned louder. I pushed her legs open and held them down. She was moving her hips up and down faster now. The next time she moved down, I tensed my tongue and positioned it in front of her pussy. When she came back up, it slid right into her wet hole. Miley shrieked and grabbed my hair with both hands, gripping tightly. I pushed my tongue deeper into her pussy and moved it around. Miley was writhing and screaming now, and I was fucking her pussy with my tongue. Although I'd been in that very same hole just a few hours ago, tasting her from the inside felt like a whole new level of intimacy.

Before long I felt her begin to shudder. I held her legs open as her pussy juices flowed around my tongue. I pulled my tongue out and went back to her clit, lapping up her juices until she became perfectly still. I lifted my head and saw Miley looking at me in half-asleep disbelief. "I have to go," I told her, "But I wanted to say bye properly."

Back home, I found Lola sleeping. She was topless and wearing a pair of my boxers. I took my clothes off and got into bed behind her. I cupped one of her beautiful breasts from behind and massaged it till she began to stir. When her eyes flew open, I pressed my hard cock against her ass. She gasped, turned to face me, and laughed, "There you are. I missed you."

I had the best girlfriend in the world. I kissed her, deeply. When we broke apart, Lola moaned "You taste like pussy."

"I thought you deserved a taste. Do you like it?"

She didn't say anything but tried to kiss me again, which I guess is a response on its own. I gave her another taste of my tongue and then held her face still. "You like the taste of Miley's pussy?" I asked her.

Lola was confused, "Miley?? But I thought Jennifer."

I wasn't in the mood to explain. "I'll tell you later" I promised. "Answer me. Do you like tasting Miley's pussy?"

Lola moaned and said, "fuck I love it. She tastes so good."

"Good girl." I took her hand and placed it on my rock-hard cock, "What're you waiting for?"

Lola groaned and practically dove down my body. She grabbed my hard dick and took it into her mouth. I placed my hands on

23

her head and pushed her slowly down till my cock was in her throat before I released her head. She jerked back, gagging a little but keeping my dick in her mouth.

I sat up so that I was sitting against the head of the bed, while Lola lay on her stomach between my legs, with a mouth full of cock. She had her eyes closed now and she didn't seem to be doing this for my sake at all. She wasn't even sucking on my cock but licking it up and down. She would start at the base and go all the way up to the tip and then lick around the head. She repeated this over every inch of my dick, clearly savoring the taste of her friend's pussy on my cock.

When she was done cleaning my dick with her tongue, she looked up at me with a satisfied, submissive expression. "Tell me everything," she said, taking just the dickhead in her mouth and sucking on it slowly.

"What was that?" I said, looking her right in the eyes. She knew the drill by now.

"I meant, please sir, would you, I want to hear how you fucked her sir. her pussy tastes so good, please sir, would you tell me everything?"

I nodded.

Lola maintained eye contact and continued sucking the whole time I described my night with Miley to her. I told her about how wet Miley had been and how tight her pussy was, how good it had felt to be inside her. I told her about Miley's tiny titties and me pulling on her nipples till she gasped. Lola suddenly shoved a hand into her shorts, clearly rubbing her pussy as she listened to me. Soon she began moaning on my dick. Lads let me tell you, if you've never made your woman moan while she's giving you head, you're missing out. I wanted to push her head down so I could fuck her throat, but I knew I wouldn't keep talking then, and she needed to hear it all.

When I got to the part about this morning and told Lola how I woke Miley up by eating her pussy, she made this low growling sound in her throat, took my dick out of her mouth, and came up to sit in my lap. She held my dick in her hand and lowered herself onto it, inserting me inch by inch into her soaking wet pussy. I groaned and finally stopped talking as she began bouncing up and down on me. I was face to face with her beautiful boobs which were bouncing wildly as she rode me. I stuck my tongue trying to lick her nipples and finally caught a large pink nipple in my mouth and sucked on it.

Lola rarely took control when we fucked, and now she was riding me like she never had before. Not used to just lying back and doing nothing while we fucked, I grabbed her hips and tried to control her momentum, but she immediately moved my hands to her tits. I squeezed them and pulled on her pretty pink nipples as she bounced on my dick.

After a minute I said something stupid like "I missed these bouncy titties" and for some reason that set her off. Lola made that soft growling sound again and threw her head back, riding me faster. I felt her pussy walls squeezing my cock as she came and that pushed me over the edge. She continued bouncing up and down, milking my dick as I came inside her. Finally, she collapsed forward into my arms and stayed there. She let my dick go soft inside her before she kissed me again and rolled off me.

Weirdly even though Lola had done all the work, I felt exhausted. Probably because I'd slept not more than 3 hours the previous night. We lay there together for a while, breathing hard and not saying a word. Lola and I had just had amazing sex because of me fucking her friend the night before. It seemed unreal. I'd also never seen her like that before, she'd been acting like a wild animal. Me coming home to her after being with another girl seemed to get her going like nothing else. I now knew for certain that Miley may have been the first, but she certainly wouldn't be the last. I held Lola close as my thoughts strayed.

Eventually, Lola interrupted my musing, "so what's up with Jennifer?" I explained what had happened and as expected Lola was immediately outraged. Not primarily because Jennifer had set me up but because she'd "kept a secret" from the other girls. Lola asked me about 3 times if I was sure I'd understood her correctly. After I told her multiple times that I'd understood Jennifer just fine, Lola grabbed her phone and ran into another room. I could hear through the door, talking angrily on the phone for about an hour while I lay in bed and thought about how weird female friendships are.

I was eating breakfast when Lola finally hung up the phone. She joined me at the table looking irritated, "Jennifer says she's sorry but I told her to save it because she's a bitch. Miley thinks I should just forget about it because that's just how Jennifer is sometimes, and we all know it. Honestly, I think she's right. I still hate her, but I guess I can't be mad forever. And Jennifer knows that which is why she pulls this shit." Lola said all this in one continuous sentence without stopping or pausing. I just stared at her, a bit amazed and not sure what I was supposed to say. She sighed and went on, "Anyway, do you want to set things up with Ekin-Su, or should I?"

Lola had asked, "Do you want to set things up with Ekin-Su, or should I?" I stared at her for a moment, processing that she'd already moved on and was planning. Now that Jennifer was out of the equation, Ekin-Su was next up on the fuck list. I thought about it for a moment and decided that I quite liked the idea of Lola "setting things up" with Ekin-Su, acting like her pimp in a way. When I told Lola that, she gave me her classic wicked smile and started texting furiously.

In the next days, this scene would repeat itself a lot: Lola's phone would buzz, she'd read a message, then look up at me and say something like "she's asking me what kind of lingerie you like". Another highlight was "you prefer shaved pussies, yeah?" It was all I could do to close my mouth and nod.

It was hard not to be flattered by the interest Ekin-Su was taking in my preferences. Although truthfully, I knew it was more about her than me. Let's talk about Ekin-Su. The truth is you know an Ekin-Su, if not in-person then definitely on social media. Picture your stereotypical sorority girl/influencer, a rich girl who is at university to party and get laid. Her #lifestyle seemed to be centered around getting and keeping people's attention. She lived for admiration, especially from guys. Knowing that her bubble butt is her biggest asset, she usually wore booty shorts or short skirts and would then revel in the attention of every guy (and girl) who stared at her.

Ekin-Su is about 5'5ft, with shoulder-length platinum blonde hair. She has Slavic, eastern-European features, I think her family was originally from Russia or Ukraine. She seemed nice enough, but I had always thought of her as a bit of a bimbo, as most of what she talked about seemed to be make-up and fitness. She claimed to be a lifestyle influencer, but her Instagram had over 10k followers and was mostly filled with photos of her showing off her ass. Not that I was complaining, especially since I now had an Instagram account. I had been missing out.

Apart from all this something else had occurred to me. When I thought about it, I realized that Lola Miley and Jennifer had created their strange rule to protect and preserve their intense childhood friendship. On the other hand, Ekin-Su was participating mostly out just out of sluttiness. now if that isn't enough to make a guy sit up and pay attention.

One of the things Ekin-Su and Lola had discussed was whether I'd be using a condom. None of us particularly wanted that and since Ekin-Su was on birth control, the consensus was that Ekin-Su, and I would both get a full STD panel. The results took a few days to come back so we'd set a date for the coming weekend.

Planning my hook-up with another girl in such detail with my girlfriend was a surreal experience, to say the least. It turned us both on like crazy and Ekin-Su's texts would often lay unanswered as I fucked Lola silly. Our kink play had also been getting more intense, with Lola wanting me to be more verbally degrading to her. She wanted me to describe in detail what I'd like to do to other girls while fucking her. We always watched porn while fucking now and she would prompt me with questions like

"Wouldn't you rather be fucking her?"

"Tell me why she's hotter than me."

"My pussy isn't enough for you, is it?"

I was initially reluctant to say such things to my wonderful girlfriend, but she wanted it and in the end, I was happy to oblige. For selfish reasons, I was also probing her attraction to the women on screen. I would tell her how she would have to lick my come off their tits or prepare another girl's pussy for me to fuck. When I said things like that she would moan like a wild animal. It was enough to make me hopeful that post-Ekin-Su I wouldn't have to return to monogamy. Although we never openly discussed it, I was becoming increasingly hopeful that Lola would someday be up for a threesome.

With these happy thoughts to keep me occupied, the rest of the week passed quickly. Soon it was time for my date with Ekin-Su. The plan was to meet at a local bar and then head back to her place. Considering that I'd never had a conversation with Ekin-Su that had lasted more than 2 minutes, I was eager to skip the bar and get to the fucking, but Ekin-Su had insisted on meeting there. Well, some liquid courage never hurt I thought. I kissed Lola goodbye first on her upper and then her lower lips. I told her I'd see her soon and the look she gave me told me she'd have her fingers in her pussy the moment I shut the door behind me.

At the bar, I got a beer and waited for Ekin-Su. Of course, she was late. The bar she'd picked was pretty fancy, it seemed to me like she was playing up the rich brat angle. I was halfway through my beer when someone put their hands over my eyes and said, "guess who". I rolled my eyes and sighed but played along, "Ekin-Su!". She giggled and took her hands away.

I leaned back to check her out. Wow. Ekin-Su had certainly dressed to impress. She was wearing a tight black dress with holes cut out on the sides to create her signature look of having her ass half-exposed. A major part of her tits was peeping out of the top of her dress, making them look much bigger than they were.

I looked her up and down appreciatively and noticed that the eyes of many of the guys she'd passed by on the way to our table were still following her, I could only imagine the view from the back. Ekin-Su seemed like she'd walked out of a magazine, airbrushed and everything. Her hair, nails, make-up, and every inch of her looked professionally done. The truth was that she did look hot but more like a doll than a real woman.

As she took her seat opposite me and leaned toward me, I

realized she was waiting for a compliment.

"Wow, Su, you look perfect," I told her honestly "like a doll". She pouted her bright pink lips, blew a kiss at me, and said, "like a fuck doll I hope".

Holy shit. I felt my dick starting to twitch in anticipation.

Su was soon drinking a fancy cocktail and talking about something or the other. My eyes had wandered back down to her pushed-up tits. She laughed, snapping me out of my thoughts "Liam, are you even listening?"

"Uhm..."

"Don't bother" she giggled, "I know where your mind is. You want to see them?"

"Hell yeah. Let's get the bill."

"No" she smiled at me, "I mean right now".

I was about to ask her what she meant but my question was soon answered as she began to roll down the top of her dress. We were right in the middle of a crowded bar, but Ekin-Su didn't seem to care. She was looking right at me as she rolled her tight dress down till her boobs were completely out in the open. All around us people were talking and drinking, and Ekin-Su had taken her breasts out for me to admire.

My dick grew harder as I stared at her small perky tits. Because of how slutty she dressed all the time, I felt like I'd seen her topless already but what I didn't know before was that through each of her pale pink nipples was a silver metal rod. Fuck, I was developing a serious thing for girls with piercings. I looked around to see that a few other people had noticed Su's little show-and-tell, they were nudging each other, and one guy was slyly filming. Su followed my gaze and saw that she had an audience. She smiled widely and turned back to me. Very deliberately she brought her hands up and pinched her nipples with her fingers while squeezing her tits together with her shoulders. It was loud in the bar, but I could have sworn I heard someone gasp.

A second later she had her top back on. I was still speechless. This girl was such an attention whore, she had my dick rock hard.

"Let's go," I said.

"Noooo, let's stay a little longer"

"I'm not asking," I told her, "Unless you plan to get completely naked here."

She smiled. Jesus, I shouldn't have given her the option.

"Wait here," she told me after we arrived at her apartment. I ignored her and pressed her against the wall. Her mouth moved willingly under mine, but she was trying to wriggle out from under me.

"Just give me a second"

"Why?"

"It'll be worth it, I promise". I sighed and let her go.

While she was gone, I looked around her apartment. Her parents were filthy rich, the apartment was in an expensive part of town and looked professionally decorated. The best part was a large balcony with a beautiful view of the city. I was starting to feel like a bit of an idiot standing alone in this apartment, so I went onto the balcony.

Ekin-Su found me there a few minutes later, "enjoying the view?"

I turned around and forgot all about the city behind me. My dick stood to attention the instant I saw her. The dress was gone. Ekin-Su was wearing absolutely nothing but a tiny thong. I groaned and kissed her, my hands going straight to her pierced tits. I pulled experimentally on the tiny metal rods, and she gasped. My hands went to my hard dick, and she expertly helped me out of my clothes. No sooner was my dick out, than she was on her knees in front of me. I moved her so I was looking out at the city as she took my dick in her mouth. The anticipation had been killing me, I groaned as she finally began sucking on my dick.

Her pale blonde hair was glinting in the dim light as she moved up and down. She was giving me an absolute porn star blowjob. She was doing these ridiculous over-the-top moans even though I wasn't touching any part of her, but her head and her spit were bubbling up and leaking all over her face as she shoved my cock in and out of her mouth. I grabbed her head and pushed my cock into her throat. For a second I heard a real gasp and then she went back to her porn star moans. Much as I was enjoying the blowjob, she was pissing me off.

"Get up," I told her.

When she stood up, I spun her around and bent her over the terrace railing. It was at rib height, so her torso and tits were hanging over the railing. We were putting on a show for any of her neighbors who happened to be watching but I was sure that that's what she would want. I shifted focus.

For the first time, I was looking at her naked ass up closely. Now I've said before that I wasn't an ass-man, but Ekin-Su's ass was a work of art. She'd taken a naturally curvy ass with potential and sculpted it into a goddamn masterpiece. Her ass cheeks were two bountiful perfect circles and I swear she'd put on some kind of lotion or something that was making her ass faintly shine and glitter in the dim light. I put my hands on it and marveled at how soft yet firm it was. I massaged her ass for a few seconds and then pushed her thong down, so it was a thin band around her knees. I spread her ass cheeks, bending her over slightly more so she was presenting me with her glistening pussy.

I was done waiting. I took my cock in my hand and positioned it. Her wet pussy accepted my cock eagerly as I slid into her. I began fucking her hard, pushing her against the railing. Su immediately began screaming and moaning, leaning over so her tits moved freely in the air.

I looked out at the city lights and then down at the beautiful girl I was fucking from behind. I grabbed her ass again and spread it, so I had better access. I was staring right at her cute pink asshole when she suddenly said in this soft high-pitched voice, "yeah daddy fuck me".

I'd never been into the whole daddy thing before but for some reason, at that moment it sent an electric volt through my body. It felt like my dick grew a couple of inches in that instant. I looked down at Ekin-Su and thought about how this was some rich guy's spoiled brat that I had bent over before me. This guy was a millionaire, and I was fucking his daughter's pussy, using her like a fuck doll.

I put one hand on Ekin-Su's waist, grabbed her by the tits, and pulled her up towards me so her back was pressed against my chest. I turned her face towards mine and began slamming into her. "What did you call me?" I growled at her.

In the same baby voice, she moaned, "Oh fuck, daddy...I need your cock, daddy."

I shoved my fingers into her filthy mouth. She immediately began sucking on them while staring into my eyes. When she had gotten each of them wet and sloppy, I pushed her away from me, bending her over again.

She kept moaning "oh daddy, oh yes daddy" as I spread her ass cheeks. I pulled my cock out so only the tip was still inside her and I positioned my thumb over her asshole. Just as she turned her head to look back at me, I rammed my cock back in at the same time as I pressed my thumb into her asshole. She screamed. For the first time that night, it was a 100% genuine scream of pleasure and shock, no acting involved. I knew what I had to do.

At first, I continued fucking her like that with my thumb moving slowly in and out of her tight asshole. She was moaning in a deeper pitch and grinding her ass against my thumb.

"You like that huh? You like my thumb in your ass?"

"Oh god yeah."

"Who are you talking to?"

"You, daddy. I love your thumb in my ass daddy..."

I pulled my thumb out and spat on my fingers. I rubbed my saliva onto her asshole slowly, pressing on it. Su was gasping and making sounds that were different now.

"Tell me what you want baby," I said. I had no idea where this was coming from, but I had fully embraced my new role.

Su groaned. She arched her back and pushed her ass up against my thumb. In her soft high-pitched voice, she moaned, "Daddy's little slut needs a cock in her ass."

Fuck. I thought I'd been ready to hear that. I pulled my cock out of her and yanked her up. "Lube?" I asked her.

"In the bedroom".

Ekin-Su ran to her bedroom, and I followed her.

"Get on all fours," I said, and she promptly obeyed.

Su scrambled onto the bed, spread her legs, and arched her back presenting both her holes to me. She was moving her ass slightly up and down like she was twerking. Such a good slut. My dick had been hard for so long now that it was aching, I shoved it into her pussy and sighed in relief. I fucked her slowly and asked her where the lube was. In the bedside table, bottom drawer Ekin-Su told me in between moans.

I leaned down and got the drawer open. Before me; were not only a variety of flavored lubes but a bunch of sex toys including a vibrator and handcuffs. I grabbed the lube and the vibrator. If Su noticed she didn't say anything. I poured a generous quantity of lube onto my dick and took some on my index and middle finger. I pushed into Su's asshole with my lubricated fingers, and she immediately collapsed face first into her pillow.

She reached behind with both hands and held her ass cheeks wide open for me. I took my fingers out and positioned my dick at her asshole. Slowly, I began to push in. As my dick pressed into her ass, I held her hips and pulled them toward me. Her asshole was so much tighter than her pussy that it felt like it was actively pushing me out. The lube was doing its job though and I kept going, slowly and deliberately until I pushed past the point of resistance. I waited till I was balls deep in her bubble butt to finally began fucking her.

I was in heaven. Although I'd had anal sex a few times before, I hadn't enjoyed it. I'd figured it wasn't really for me and I was more than satisfied with pussy. Since Lola had had her own bad experience with anal, we'd never even bothered to try it.

But fucking Su in the ass was a whole different experience. Her ass was the tightest grip I'd ever felt on my dick. Every time I slid my dick out, it felt like I wouldn't get back inside. But I kept pushing in and out of her slippery asshole. Her bountiful ass was jiggling with every thrust. I wanted to grab her ass cheeks and shake them, but Su had a tight grip on them. She was spreading her ass wide open as she gasped and moaned like no sounds I'd ever heard from her before. All her performances seemed to have disappeared as she had pulled her cheeks apart for me.

Now she was twerking her ass and whimpering "daddy, daddy" in a soft moan each time my balls slapped against her.

I reached down and pulled gently on one of her nipples piercing. She moaned louder, "oh god yes, give it to me daddy".

I felt myself getting close to coming. I grabbed the vibrator and positioned it under her clit. I pulled my dick out and I turned the vibrator on just as I slammed my dick back into her asshole. Su shrieked and began shaking violently. Her asshole's death grip on me impossibly seemed to tighten even more and I began to cum. I continued fucking her as I shot my come deep into her ass and held the vibrator at her clit until Su's screams had stopped. Finally, I pulled out and surveyed the scene before me. Su had collapsed face down into the pillows, her ass was still in the air and had me cum leaking out of it.

I massaged her ass cheeks gently and rubbed her back before getting into bed next to her. Su's face looked ruined, her make-up was all over the pillows and her mascara had smeared all around her eyes. I kissed her gently and asked if she was okay.

She looked at me through watering eyes and said, "thank you for fucking my ass daddy".

I wanted to give the girl a damn medal.

In the cab home I felt simultaneously on-top-of-the-world and strangely melancholic. I had now fucked two of my girl-friend's best friends. Incredible. But although it had been amazing, it was now over, and I hadn't scored the trifecta. Impulsively, I took my phone out and pulled up Jennifer's Insta-gram. I had been scrolling through her photos absentmindedly for a few minutes when I realized that I had accidentally liked one of her older pictures at some point. I immediately removed my like but a second later I got a notification from Jennifer. She had followed me. Shit, she knew I was stalking her in the middle of the night. Ugh, I'd never stop making a fool of myself with this girl.

To my surprise, she immediately followed up with a message "You're up late (; how's it going?"

Jennifer had never texted me before. The embarrassment was making me feel hot under my collar. While I was thinking about what to do, the cab stopped, and I realized I was back home. I left her on read and went upstairs. There I found Lola awake and waiting for me. I'd barely gotten out a "hey" before she was down on her knees, fumbling with my jeans, trying to get my dick out. I stopped her and tried to pull her up, but she was in wild animal mode.

She looked confused for a moment and then her face cleared, she immediately began rambling "please sir, let me suck your dick. I want to taste Su's pussy sir."

I laughed and helped her stand up. I kissed her and said, "you probably don't want to taste her ass though".

Lola's face was a mask of shock. "You, you fucked her ass?"

"Fuck yeah I did; it was so hot baby."

Lola's mouth snapped shut. She suddenly seemed furious. She wrenched free of my grasp and ran to the bedroom, slamming the door shut behind her.

I was at a loss. I had had no idea that anal had been off-limits. Come to think of it we'd never discussed any rules or boundaries, which is why I had assumed there weren't any. Now I'd upset the world's greatest girlfriend, I felt horrible. I took a shower and spent the rest of the night on the couch.

When I woke up the next day, Lola was tucked under my arm sleeping next to me on the couch. When I stirred, she woke up and kissed me deeply. I had a feeling I wasn't in trouble anymore. "I'm sorry Liam, I just got, I guess, jealous.". I hugged her and told her it was completely understandable, and I hadn't meant to upset her.

"It's just that... you never seemed interested in my ass."

"Are you kidding? I'd love to fuck that cute little ass" I reached behind her to squeeze the ass in question.

Lola was burrowing into my arms, hiding her face now. "No, you wouldn't. Su's ass is so much better. You wouldn't want mine. "

"No, stop that. Of course, I–"

Lola wouldn't even let me get the whole thing out. She interrupted, "I bet the only way you could fuck my ass is if you were looking at hers."

OH. I paused and reassessed the mood she was in. I tentatively reached into her panties and when my fingers touched her pussy, they were soaked. Wow. I gently rubbed her clit and waited for her to say something else.

After a few long moments of silence, I took the leap of faith, "I think you're right." I told her slowly, "so why don't we invite her to join us?"

Lola moaned and raised her face to kiss me.

I had just taken the leap and suggested to my girlfriend Lola that we invite her friend Su to join us in bed. Amazingly, Lola responded by moaning and kissing me. Just a few hours ago Lola had been furious when I told her I'd fucked Su in the ass. And now my fingers were pressed against her drenched pussy as Lola moaned at the thought of me fucking her while staring at her best friend's ass. Talk about a reversal of fortunes.

I kissed my girlfriend back, thrown by the rapid turn of events. I wasn't sure if she was serious about having a threesome with Su or was just guilty about the way she'd reacted last night. As I tried to untangle that thought, my brain conjured up an incredible image of Su and Lola making out with my cock in between their lips. Fuck. I needed to make this happen. Instinctively, I pulled Lola closer and pressed my hard cock against her stomach. She gasped, grinding against me.

I pulled back and rubbed her clit gently, watching her writhe in pleasure. Desperate for her to say it out loud, I kissed up her neck and whispered in her ear, "Do you want Su to join us?"

She gave a soft moan and nodded a little but kept her eyes closed. My heart began to beat faster.

I slipped a finger into her drenched pussy and elicited a moan. "Tell me what you want" I ordered. With her eyes still closed, she whispered, "I want to hear how you fucked her sir."

Fuck. Of course. I yanked Lola's t-shirt off, so I had a good view of her breasts jiggling slightly as I began to describe my evening with Su. I fingered Lola slowly as I told her about how slutty Su had been, getting her tits out in the bar. I pinched Lola's pink nipples when I described Su's nipple piercings and how I pulled on them to make her moan. When I got to the part about bending Su over the balcony rail, Lola's eyes flew open.

I took my hand out of her panties and put my fingers in her mouth, making her taste herself as I told her about how Ekin-Su had called me Daddy. Lola's eyes were wide as she listened, moaning on my fingers. Her hands went to the bulge in my shorts. She pulled my dick out and began stroking me frantically as I described how I fucked Su's pussy.

I was desperate to get my cock inside Lola, but the stakes were high, and I made myself focus on Lola's pleasure. I noticed that Lola moaned whenever I told her how slutty Su was, so I described in detail how she had been behaving like a porn star, with her over-the-top moans and the way she had sucked my dick.

At this point, my cock had begun to throb. My super sexy memories of Su combined with the sight of my girlfriend getting off on them, meant I wouldn't be lasting much longer. I pushed Lola's hands away from my cock, took my fingers out of her mouth, and flipped her on her stomach. She turned on her side to look back at me in confusion and began to say, "What?" Before she could get it out, I spanked her. Hard. She moaned and arched her back. I yanked her panties down, pulled her ass up toward me, and slammed two fingers back into her pussy. Lola screamed and trembled as I fingered her.

"You want to hear how I fucked Su's ass don't you?" I spoke.

"Fuck, yes, I do" she groaned.

"Yes, what?!"

"Yes sir, please sir. I want to know how you fucked Su's ass."

I pulled my fingers out of her pussy and spread her ass cheeks. As I stared at her perfect little asshole, I found it hard to believe I hadn't fucked it already. I brought my fingers to it. Lola had cried out in protest as my fingers left her pussy, but her protest soon turned to a gasp as she felt me spreading her wetness on her asshole.

I gently pressed my index finger into her pink rosebud. Lola screamed and shuddered, but she pressed her face into the sofa, raising her ass to meet me. Her asshole was unbelievably tight, even more so than Su's. I wiggled my finger up to the first digit and Lola was moaning incoherently. Unable to take it anymore, I positioned my dick in front of her pussy and pushed in.

I groaned in relief as I finally started fucking her pussy. I spanked her again and brought my finger back to her asshole, pushing it in slowly.

As I thrusted, I told her, "Imagine my cock was in your ass instead of your pussy. That's what Su got to experience." Lola moaned again and shuddered as I pushed my finger deeper into her tight asshole.

Before long I felt her pussy clench on my cock, and I began to shoot my come into her. After I finished, I pulled out and collapsed backward.

Lola remained completely still, her ass still in the air. I pulled her up towards me onto my lap. She was looking at me with this strange expression on her face, it was a mix between shyness, lust, and wonder. I kissed her and waited for her to say something, it was strange for her to be so quiet. Finally, I said, "so do you still think I'm not interested in your ass?"

"No," she shook her head and laughed.

I smiled and teased her, "but your ass is so tight. I don't know if it can take my cock."

She looked up at me with a wicked smile and said, "I'll ask Su to help."

Fuck yeah.

As you can imagine, I spent the next few days walking on clouds as I waited for the plans to be made. Although the actual business of Lola asking Su hadn't happened yet, now that I knew that Lola was definitely on board, I was certain this was going to happen. I was sure that Su wouldn't say no to an offer like this, not to mention that she'd probably find it very flattering.

As to what exactly the offer was, I wasn't very clear. Whenever Lola and I talked about it, by which I mean, loudly fantasized about it during sex, Lola spoke about it in terms of Su 'helping me' fuck Lola in the ass.

Didn't sound exactly like a typical threesome but I could hardly be disappointed. A few days later, Lola told me that she'd talked to Su and Su had agreed to help. My dick immediately began to twitch, and Lola was practically ripping off my clothes as she

41

told me this.

But since it was now certain that my dreams would be coming true, I decided it was time to finally clarify what exactly Lola was picturing. She wasn't straightforward about these things, but I didn't want any misunderstandings. When I asked Lola, sure enough, she seemed slightly annoyed and she said, "I don't want to plan everything."

"But I need to know what you want, I don't want to accidentally upset you", I told her.

Finally, he took a deep breath and said, "I know you want her more than me, but you'll be fucking my ass not hers".

"You know that's not true" I tried to tell her that I was just trying to avoid a misunderstanding, but she just got more annoyed.

Finally, she sighed and said that I could touch Su but not fuck her. I was disappointed to hear it, but I nodded. Honestly with everything Lola had given me I had no right to be disappointed. Besides, by the sound of it, my fantasy of a double blowjob was still going to be fulfilled.

I kissed Lola and told her I understood completely. But she still seemed irritated. I was mystified but wasn't getting anywhere so I changed the topic.

Su would be out of town for the next week, so the date had been set for the next weekend. There was certainly enough time for the anticipation to grow but Lola kept sending me mixed signals.

On one hand, she seemed extremely turned on by the idea of bringing another girl into our bed. We'd been fantasizing about it abstractly for a while now. Ever since she first revealed her cuckquean fetish to me, we'd begun watching porn as we fucked. And we'd discovered that what drove her particularly crazy was making me compare her body to the girls on screen.

She would prompt me with questions like, "Wouldn't you rather be fucking her right now?" Or "Her tits are so much bigger than mine, aren't they?"

After some initial hesitation, I got into the flow of describing in detail what I'd do to those other girls while ravaging my sexy girlfriend. Lola had explained her cuckquean fetish in terms of wanting to be with an alpha man. But although she never explicitly said it, the jealousy and humiliation seemed to be part of what got her off.

Ever since my encounter with Su, the unbelievable sexiness of this scenario had now been compounded by the fact that the girl she wanted to be compared to was Su. Although Lola had initially responded with anger and jealousy, she now seemed insanely turned on by the fact that I had fucked Su's ass before hers.

Now when we fucked, I'd often finger her ass and she'd say things like, "My ass is going to be disappointing to you after Su's." And "It's going to be so hard for you to fuck my ass when Su's is right there." It was enough to make me feel like I was walking through a minefield. I'd make some non-committal response and then she'd say, "her ass deserves your come more than mine."

Wtf? On one hand, holy fuck is that hot. On the other hand, my anticipation for the threesome was souring a little because I was unsure what Lola wanted.

And I didn't want to ask again and risk putting her off the whole thing. With just a few days to go, I texted Su to see if Lola had been more candid with her about what she wanted. Ekin-Su's reply was uncharacteristically short and to the point, "She wants you to push her boundaries ;) "

Reading Ekin-Su's text was a eureka moment. Of course, I thought, Lola had always indicated to me that she wanted to be dominated. In my attempt to be considerate, I'd been ignoring what she was telling me indirectly. Ideally, we would be able to have an open discussion about what we each preferred but if Lola wasn't up for that, this was the next best thing.

Once Ekin-Su had cleared some of the fog, my anticipation began building again. I could hardly believe what I was going to be experiencing in just a few days. Naturally, I was once again spending a lot of time at the gym. All the time that is, that I didn't spend on Lola. Apart from giving her a lot of time and attention, we had also been slowly training her tight asshole for D-day. At first, I'd been barely able to wiggle my index finger up to the knuckle but now with the help of lube and some perseverance, I could comfortably squeeze my thumb into her ass which I now did every time we fucked. The key was to take it slow. I had learned from Lola that her only previous attempt at anal had gone bad when the dude had tried to just shove his cock in without warming her up properly. Rookie mistake lads, slow and steady wins more than just races.

As part of our preparation, Lola and I visited a sex store to pick up a few items we figured might come in handy. Specifically, we were looking to buy water-based lube and a new vibrator, but I was secretly hoping to purchase a double-sided dildo. Unsurprisingly, I'd been watching a lot more threesome porn recently and something new I'd discovered that I enjoyed was two chicks using a double-sided dildo together while sucking dick. I mean. yeah, that's pretty explanatory. That's hot as fuck. I was aware however that for my first ever threesome, this was flying too close to the sun. Sure, enough at the store when I half-jokingly pointed out the double-sided dildos Lola gave me an odd look, laughed and turned away. One thing at a time, I told myself. I would have to wait a bit longer before I fulfilled that fantasy, but that's a story for another day.

In the meantime, we purchased a new vibrator, lots of water-based lube and ended up picking up a jeweled butt plug as well. Lola was bright pink and excited by the time we left the cute store. I was used to my confident, self-assured girlfriend but lately, I was seeing this whole new side of her, shyer and wanting me to take the lead also outside of the bedroom. Ever since I'd talked with Ekin-Su about it, I had started being more assertive with Lola in the bedroom and the results were incredible.

When we fantasized about our upcoming threesome during sex, instead of being confused by Lola's mixed signals, I would now tell her how she was going to watch me fuck her friend. Her response to this was invariably going into wild animal mode and fucking me silly. Afterwards, she never brought it up nor revised her instructions about the actual threesome. I still didn't know what was going to happen on the day, but I figured I would have to play it by ear.

Even if I didn't end up fucking Su again, I'd still be having the experience of a lifetime with two total babes, and I was more than okay with that.

Finally, THE day was here. Lola had spent all day exfoliating, moisturizing and God knows what else. By the time the evening rolled around, Lola finally came out of the bathroom looking as dolled up as Su always did. She was wearing a simple white dress that showed off her boobs and ended a little above her knees. She even had light make-up on. She asked me anxiously how she looks, and it hit me that she'd done all this not mainly to impress me but Su. I wasn't sure how intimate Lola planned to get with Su but seeing that she was trying to impress her was making my cock twitch in anticipation.

"You look beautiful," I told her honestly. I'd been paying her a lot of attention and showering her with compliments lately, not only because she genuinely was an amazing girlfriend but also because I wanted to stave off any potential jealousy she felt. Looking at her now, I seem to have succeeded because I saw pure excitement on her face. I pulled her into my lap and had begun to kiss her when the doorbell rang, and Lola practically ran to answer it.

Su was not late for once. Lola and I weren't the only ones looking forward to this. Once the squealing and hugs had subsided, I got a proper look at Su. Of course, she was as perfectly made up as ever. Her hair hung straight and loose and she was wearing high-waist booty denim shorts and a tight tube top. Pretty tame stuff for Su but the fact that I could make out her pierced nipples through the thin fabric made up for that. I greeted her with a hug. There was a little awkwardness in the air mingled with the sexual tension as I hadn't seen her since we'd fucked at her place.

Su was smiling at me with a knowing look, and it occurred to me that this was very probably not her first threesome. My cock twitched again in anticipation, and I took a deep breath.

Both girls were waiting for me to say something. Eventually, I blurted out, "Does anyone want a drink?"

That broke the ice, and everyone laughed a little at the strangeness of the situation as I prepared our drinks. We talked a little about random things as we slowly let the alcohol go to our heads. I was not paying attention to the conversation but silently brainstorming ways to get this party started.

I caught only snatches of the conversation as I tuned in and out. ...crazy place...so rich...lucky bitch...at his beach house...too bad he's bad in bed.

Wait, what? I tuned back into the conversation.

"Who's bad in bed?" I asked and the girls burst out laughing.

"Jennifer's new boyfriend," Su told me. "Apparently, he's hot and rich but sadly, doesn't have a lot going for him downstairs…" She shrugged and winked at me, "Most guys only have two out of three." Lola giggled.

This information was both gratifying and irritating to me, I couldn't say exactly why. I hadn't thought about Jennifer in a while, and I'd also been off Instagram. I asked the girls where she'd been lately. They sighed wistfully and informed me that she was currently on a long holiday with her boyfriend at his fancy beach villa. Apparently, whenever she wasn't showing off and trying to make her friends envious, she was complaining about her boyfriend to them. This sounded like the Jennifer I knew. Thinking about her using this unsuspecting guy was pissing me off as much as the thought of him getting to fuck her.

I was getting annoyed, so I went to the kitchen to fix myself another drink and clear my head. When I got back, Lola and Su were giggling and talking softly. Su whispered something in Lola's ear and Lola giggled and nodded. "What's going on?" I asked. "Oh nothing, we're just talking about how Jennifer would be jealous if she knew what she was missing out on," Lola said with a slightly drunken grin on her face.

I didn't know what to say to that, so I just stood there and sipped my drink. Su was slowly stroking Lola's hair. I thought the time had come to make a move. I went over to them and sat next to them on the large couch. The girls started giggling again and I noticed that Lola and Su were holding hands. I leaned over and kissed Lola. She kissed me back eagerly and cupped my face with her free hand.

I felt another hand on my lower back. My heart began beating faster, this was happening! I began to rub Lola's tits lightly over her dress. She pulled back and smiled at me nervously.

Hardly a second passed before Su leaned forward and kissed Lola. The kiss was slow and sensual for a few moments and then they were aggressively making out with each other. I watched in awe as these two insanely hot girls tasted each other's tongues in front of me.

My cock was straining against my jeans at this point. Su was pulling Lola's dress over her head, revealing her matching white bra and panties. I went behind Lola to assist her, and took Lola's bra off, leaving her topless.

I had barely grabbed her breasts from behind when Su already had one of Lola's nipples in her mouth and was sucking on it. Lola began moaning softly. Holy shit. Nothing had happened for a long time and then suddenly a lot was happening very quickly.

The sight of Su sucking on Lola's tits and making her moan was incredible. I wanted to touch Su, but I made myself focus on Lola first. She was now sandwiched between me and Su on the couch, wearing only her panties. As Su moved from one pink nipple to the other, I reached into Lola's panties.

Unsurprisingly, she was wet. I began rubbing her clit and she moaned louder, "oh my god. Oh my god."

Su took this as a call to action and began making out with her again. I pushed Lola's panties down to her knees and continued flicking her clit. She had her eyes closed as she moaned and bucked against my fingers. I couldn't resist any longer, with my free hand I leaned forward and groped Su's tits over her tank top. She immediately paused from making out and pulled her top off.

She was wearing nothing underneath. I now had one hand on my girlfriend's wet pussy with the other gently pulling on Su's pierced nipples. They were both moaning into each other's mouths as they kissed.

Incredible as the visual stimuli was, my cock was practically aching by now. I was considering unbuttoning my jeans when I saw that Su was now kissing her way down Lola's body. Hell yeah.

Her lips were at my finger which was still rubbing circles on Lola's clit. I watched as she stared at her friend's bare pussy close for the first time. I felt Lola jolt and I knew she had opened her eyes and was looking at Su's face between her legs. Lola's legs instinctively tried to close, but I immediately tightened my grip on her thigh with one hand, holding her legs apart. She whimpered.

My finger dipped down and slightly entered her wet hole. A moan escaped Lola as her body jerked again. At the same moment, Su looked up into my eyes with an expression of pure lust. She then bent forward and took Lola's clit in her mouth. Lola began to tremble and scream. I could feel Su's lips and tongue against my finger before I moved my hand away and began to massage Lola's tits. Su was eating Lola out, licking her pussy frantically and occasionally pausing to suck on her clit. Holy shit the girl was a professional. It was clear to all involved that Su was certainly no amateur when it came to pussy eating.

I watched her in awe as Lola began to shudder in my arms. She had one hand in Su's hair, holding her close as she trembled and came hard.

Unable to take it anymore, as soon as Lola came, my hands went to my rock-hard cock. I unbuttoned and unzipped my jeans. Lola was lying back and panting, she had her eyes closed and

Su was still slowly licking her inner folds. When she heard me unzip my pants, she raised her head, and I immediately pulled her up towards me. I kissed her, tasting Lola's pussy on her mouth. Her hands immediately went to my cock, pulling my boxers down and taking my hard dick out. I groaned in relief as she wrapped her hand around my dick and began to stroke it.

She climbed off the couch and got on her knees on the ground before me, still stroking my cock. I felt Lola pulling my t-shirt off from behind me. She kissed my back and then crawled over to the couch, joining Su kneeling in front of me.

I grabbed Lola's head and pushed her toward my dick. She began slowly licking the dick head and immediately Su followed her lead and began licking the other side of my dick. I felt like I'd died and gone to heaven. The two beautiful blondes were licking up and down my dick, worshipping every inch of it. Su began to make her trademark porn star noises, spit bubbling up all over her face. Lola was licking and sucking along the base and shaft while Su was sucking on my dick head. I grabbed her head and pushed her down on my dick. She moaned louder and took my dick into her throat. Fuck.

I began thrusting myself into her throat when I suddenly looked to the side and noticed Lola's expression. She was watching me throat fuck Ekin-Su with an expression of pure desire on her face. Her eyes were unfocused, and her mouth was open as she watched. I grabbed her head and pulled her back towards my dick. She immediately began licking my balls as Su worked my cock. After a few minutes of this, I began to feel my cock pulsating and with a great effort, I pulled Su off my dick.

Uncomfortable as it was having my cock back out in the cold air, my head was swimming, and I needed a small break if I was going to last. The two girls looked at me expectantly. "Make out on my cock," I told them. Lola and Su grinned at each other. Lola put one hand on my cock and brought it between their lips. They began to make out. Fuck. The sensation of them kissing with my cock between their lips and their thrashing tongues was everything I had hoped it would be. I was immediately addicted. I could have stayed like that forever and I would have been happy.

After what felt like too short a time, Lola raised her head and said, "fuck please fuck me."

I was reluctant to leave my personal heaven, but my throbbing cock also needed release. I looked at Lola and then at Su. I remembered what Su had told me about Lola. I turned away from Lola.

"Take off your shorts," I told Su.

She seemed a little surprised but stood up and obeyed. Underneath she had on a tiny orange thong that barely covered her pussy.

"Turn around," I told her, and she did, revealing her amazing ass which had swallowed up the string.

Lola was watching this silently. I could see how turned on she was. I reached out and grabbed Su's ass, shaking it so it jiggled. I spanked it lightly and Su let out a soft moan. I looked at Lola and said, "do you deserve to be fucked before her?"

Lola gasped. I waited with bated breath. Her shock melted away and then she said, "I, I don't."

"You don't what?"

"I don't... deserve to be fucked before her, sir," Su twisted around to look at us, looking amazed. For a girl like Su this was playing perfectly into her kinks as well.

"Good girl. I'm going to fuck her in our bed." I told Lola and led Su by hand to the bedroom. There she scrambled onto the bed on all fours, just as she had done last time. She bent her bubble butt up in the air before me. Lola followed us to the bedroom and sat next to us on the bed. I was about to fuck Su in front of my girlfriend. Lola was breathing heavily, and I decided to push my luck even further.

"Tell me what you want Lola."

"Oh fuck."

"Say it. I want Su to hear."

"Oh god, please fuck her sir. I want to watch you fuck her."

Su moaned.

"Why?" I asked Lola. I could see from her face that she was uncomfortable but that very discomfort was turning her on. I was determined to push her boundaries. I smiled at her.

"Why do you want to watch me fuck her?" I said again.

"Because she's so fucking hot sir..." She trailed off. I simply stared at her. I rubbed my cock on Su's pussy, waiting. Lola hesitated for a moment and then panted, "because she deserves your cock sir... she deserves it more than I do."

As she soon said the last part, I shoved my cock in. Su practically screamed as I pushed into her wet pussy. I began to fuck her fast, and Lola groaned and slipped a hand between her legs.

She scrambled towards us for a good view. She ended up kneeling next to me and watching as my dick slammed in and out of Su. I tried to kiss Lola as I fucked Su, but she pulled away almost immediately, her eyes fixed on my dick. Clearly, she wanted to watch.

Alright then, I thought and yanked her forward, so her cheek was pressed against Su's ass, and she had a perfect view of my dick entering her friend's pussy.

I slammed my dick hard into Su's hole. She began panting "oh yeah, oh yeah," repeatedly in this high-pitched porno voice as I fucked her. Finally, my cock began to pulse, and I felt the release course through my body as I finally began to cum. I kept thrusting into her, shooting a huge load into Su's pussy as she moaned and screamed so loudly, that I was sure our neighbors could hear.

As soon as I finished coming, I pulled out and Lola grabbed my cock and began sucking on it. I guess she finally got to taste Su's pussy on my cock. As Lola was devouring my cock, Su turned over onto her back. I made eye-contact with her, she was panting as she watched Lola clean my cock.

After a few moments, I gently guided her face towards Su's dripping pussy. I knew that before today, Lola's girl-on-girl action had been limited to kissing and touching. But today was a day for firsts.

Lola looked up at me and I nodded, encouraging her. She leaned forward and began licking Su's pussy. Su closed her eyes and whimpered in a way I'd never heard before. It was unbelievably sexy.

Now that I had cum, I was once again clear-headed enough to appreciate just how incredible this situation was. Lola was slowly eating my cum out of Su's creampied pussy. Wow. I took a few moments to admire the view, then I picked up the lube from the bedside table and scooped a generous amount of it up with my fingers.

I got off the bed, stood behind Lola who was engrossed in her task, and spread her ass. She gasped which made Su whimper again and Lola continued licking her wet pussy. I massaged the lube into Lola's puckered rosebud, and she began moaning against Su's clit. Su now had her legs wrapped around Lola's head.

I gently slipped a finger into my girlfriend's asshole as Su came against her face. I watched Su's face as she came, her face was scrunched up and her mouth was open. Free from her usual play-acting, she looked vulnerable and real. And truth be told, even sexier than usual.

I shifted focus to Lola's ass. It was so tight; I could feel her inner walls squeezing my finger. I slowly eased another finger into her and she arched her back and began panting. Su was now murmuring softly to her and rubbing her shoulders.

Suddenly she said, "not like this baby, turn around."

I pulled my fingers out of Lola's asshole and she got on her back with her head in Su's lap. She spread her legs and raised her ass. I bent down to kiss her stomach before shifting my attention back to her ass. I gently worked my fingers back in and began to finger Lola's ass slowly until her whimpers turned to moans.

Needlessly to say my cock was hard again. I pushed it into Lola's soaking wet pussy, and she squealed. I fucked her pussy slowly while still fingering her ass, now with my thumb. I was completely lost in the moment when out of nowhere, Su grabbed her phone and snapped a picture of my dick entering Lola. "What the fuck?" I exclaimed but Su just winked at me. Lola didn't even react, she was too overwhelmed by all the sensations. I focused on the task at hand. Finally, I pulled my dick out of Lola's pussy and positioned it at her ass. Su handed me the lube again and I slathered it generously on my dick. I looked Lola in the eyes and asked, "are you ready?" She nodded and leaned back in Su's lap. I began to push very slowly into Lola's asshole.

At first, it seemed like there was no way her ass would accept my dick. But I continued to push slowly, and Su pulled Lola's legs back toward her, giving me a better angle. Slowly, very slowly, my cock began to sink into her asshole. I watched Lola's face carefully; she was trembling and had her eyes closed but seemed to be enjoying the sensation. After many minutes passed, I was fully inside her ass. The feeling was unbelievable. Her asshole was so tight it felt like it was crushing my dick. Eventually, I began to move inside her, slowly fucking her asshole.

Lola was moaning loudly now, gasping incoherently. Su stroked her hair and face and rubbed her neck and shoulders. Seeing how much Su cared for Lola was making me feel very affectionate towards her. We made eye contact as I slid in and out of Lola's ass, and Su blew me a kiss.

It was so fucking sexy to stare at Su, lingering on her pierced tits as I fucked my girlfriend in the ass. My gaze switched between Su's face and tits and Lola's beautiful body spread out in front of me. Su was massaging Lola's breasts now, pinching her nipples between her forefinger and thumb as I slid in and out of her.

I gradually increased my pace, going faster and spending slightly longer with my balls pressed against Lola's ass each time I was fully inside her. Finally, when I was ready to come, I closed my eyes and upped my pace even more. I heard a buzzing sound and opened my eyes to see that Su had placed the vibrator on Lola's clit. Genius. I had completely forgotten about the toys. Lola was shaking now, and I began fucking her harder. She screamed incoherently as I finally pumped my come into her ass.

Su kept the vibrator on Lola's clit for a little longer after I'd pulled out. I watched as Su expertly rubbed the sex toy on her friend's pussy until she came again, shuddering violently. Exhausted, we all collapsed in a heap onto the bed. Su and I stroked and kissed Lola, who was in between us until she seemed to recover. I couldn't believe how well everything had worked out.

I'd just had the most incredible experience of my life and I had Su to thank not only for her heads up about what Lola wanted but for being so generous and cool during the threesome. After resting for a bit Lola went off to take a shower, leaving Ekin-Su and me alone.

I turned to see Su watching me with a sly smile playing on her lips. Truth be told, I wanted to kiss her. I wanted to grab her magnificent ass and spread it. I wanted to push her onto her back and make her whimper as she had before. I wanted to watch her face as she came around my cock. The way Su was looking at me I thought she knew what I was thinking. Although she was still naked and in my bed, something told me that ravaging Su now would be out of bounds.

Instead, I impulsively leaned forward and kissed her. Nothing wild, just a short, sweet kiss. Su kissed me back for a few moments and I pulled back, not wanting to get carried away. She still had that wicked smile on her face.

I thanked Su and told her I couldn't be more grateful to her for everything. She simply laughed and said, "I bet you could." At the time I just laughed with her and didn't think much of it.

But a few days later, when I had resigned myself to the fact that life would be downhill from here on out, my phone buzzed. It was a photo from Ekin-Su, a cropped screenshot of texts between her and Jennifer. It was the picture she had taken of me, and Lola followed by a message from Jennifer, "ugh, I need that cock so bad right now."

I had been sitting in bed with my laptop open, working while my girlfriend slept beside me. A perfectly ordinary night that had just been turned upside down by Su's text. I was now staring speechless at the screenshot Su had sent me. It was the picture she had taken of me and Lola during our threesome, followed by a message from Jennifer, "ugh, I need that cock so bad right now."

The cock in question was already beginning to respond to those words. I was just thinking about what to say when my phone buzzed again.

Another text from Su: "I told you she'd be jealous. Your move ;)"

Wow. I read Jennifer's message a few more times. A part of me was still suspicious of her, after the way she had treated me before. I wasn't planning on making a fool of myself again. On the other hand, there was the hottest girl I'd ever seen in real life confessing that she wanted to fuck me. If there was ever a time to throw caution to the wind.

I should've been clearing my head but instead, I did the exact opposite and pulled up Jennifer's Insta. It had been a while since I'd checked it last and I saw that she hadn't posted anything new. Strange, since as far as I knew she was still at her rich boyfriend's beach house and usually didn't miss an opportunity to show off.

I scrolled up and down her familiar feed aimlessly for a few seconds before coming back to the last pic Jennifer had posted. She was standing on a boat, looking off to the side wearing a red and gold bikini that looked incredible on her caramel skin. It was hard to believe this was a person I knew in real life and not a magazine centerfold.

Looking at her face with its perfect delicate features, it was hard to remember what a bitch she could be. And looking at her body... it was hard to remember my name. My eyes seemed glued to her breasts, which her bikini top was struggling to contain. For the millionth time, I imagined what they would look like bare, in my palms. I took a deep breath and double-tapped on the image, liking it.

Almost immediately, there was a new tile on her feed. And then another. And yet another. Each photo is more heartbreaking than the last. What was happening? Surely these weren't for my benefit? I opened my DM's and realized that I had never responded to Jennifer's last messages. I bet that didn't happen to her often.

My working theory was that the combination of my apparent disinterest as well as whatever stories Su had been telling Jennifer had been a winning formula. I couldn't help but laugh, it seemed so juvenile. I decided to toy with her a little. Assuming that my conjectures were correct, it would be the right thing to do. And in case this was all still one of her games, I would still be playing it safe.

I went back to her profile, liked all her new photos and then really gave each of them my full attention. Her tiny bikinis got smaller and smaller each time. I absently wondered how she walked around in those tiny scraps of fabric without them giving out under the strain. This train of thought as well as the assorted boats, beaches, and hot tubs in the backdrop of her images were fueling my fantasies.

However, my happy thoughts were rudely interrupted by the irritating realization that she was being fucked in those places regularly by the bastard rich enough to take her there.

It was at this moment of being half annoyed and half extremely turned on that Jennifer sent me a text. It said, "So you can like my pictures but can't reply to me?" I laughed, amazed at how the tables had turned.

Here was this gorgeous woman I'd been lusting over for the better part of a year, and she was seeking validation from me.

Before I could write back, she'd sent another text "at least I know you like what you see".

It was on.

I won't bore you all with the details of our texts but suffice it to say that I now had Jennifer's number, both literally and metaphorically. Much as it killed me to play the long game, the more nonchalant I was, the more she wanted my validation. She wasn't great at the banter, but I guess when a girl looks like Jennifer does, she doesn't have to be. We flirted back and forth for a few hours until she eventually said, "btw I really am sorry about that day at the club...I know you were really disappointed." I made myself take a deep breath and count to 10 before responding, "I was but it was probably for the best."

"What do you mean??" She shot back.

"No offense but I don't think you're my type in bed," I wrote back, terrified I was overplaying my hand.

"What's your type in bed?" She asked.

"I'm sure Su has told you."

"I don't know what you mean"

At this point I didn't know what else to say, I was beginning to lose the thread a bit. But my indecision proved to be perfectly complementary to Jennifer's impatience. My phone buzzed again and under Jennifer's name were the words "I can be obedient. If that's what you're looking for." Fuck yeah.

Me: I doubt that.

Jennifer: I can.

Me: so, you're saying you want to obey me?

After a long pause during which I stopped being an atheist

Jennifer: yes

My breath quickened as I considered the possibilities before me. I was now 99% sure that I would get to fuck the girl of my dreams. but then again Jennifer was so fickle. I made up my mind.

A boob in hand is worth two in the bush. I was done waiting.

"Then take your top off" I texted.

I waited a few minutes, counting Lola's even breaths beside me. Finally, finally, I was rewarded.

Holy. Fuck. If she hadn't already made me become a believer, this would have done it. I must have replayed that clip half a hundred times, memorizing the outline of the huge light brown areolas, the perfect bounce of her perfect breasts. They were somehow better than I'd imagined.

I texted her back slower, as I was now typing with one hand. Suppressing the urge to compose sonnets about her breasts, I said "You were wearing that at 2 am? Planning to go swimming?"

"I put it on so I could take it off for you" came the reply.

Any damage Jennifer had done to my ego was completely undone. My cock was now hard as a rock. Part of me desperately wanted to wake Lola up and fuck her silly but I couldn't possibly stop texting Jennifer now.

"Good girl. Leave it off, you're going swimming. Go to the hot tub." I instructed her.

"Now???"

I didn't respond. Several minutes later, I got another clip. Fuck. It was too much. I reached under Lola's t-shirt. I sighed in relief as I grabbed one of her breasts in my palm. She stirred slightly but her breathing remained even. I moved her body towards me so I could continue staring at the clip Jennifer had sent me as I gently massaged my girlfriend's breasts. Lola stirred again and blinked, "What-?" I tossed my phone aside and slid down so I could kiss her. As her mouth opened for me, I slipped a hand into her panties. She was soon moaning against my lips.

I was sure Lola didn't know what had brought this on, but I was also sure that just then she didn't care. She reached for my cock and gasped when she felt how hard I was. I yanked her T-shirt up and began to suck on her nipples. The image of Jennifer's incredible Double D's bouncing in the water was seared into the backs of my eyelids. When Lola moaned again, I flipped her on her stomach and pulled her shorts down.

I spread her ass, lined my cock up against her wet pussy, and thrust into her. I didn't start slow, instead fucking her hard, prone bone, with my hand pressing down on the small of her back. Lola let out a groan and began panting, "please sir, fuck me, sir. Use my hole."

This set me off. "You're my fuck doll", I told her as I slammed into her.

Lola began screaming in agreement, "I'm your fuck doll, sir, please keep using me, sir."

I groaned and upped the pace. Lola twisted around to look back at me.

When she lifted her head, I realized that my phone was right next to her face. This gave me the kind of idea that you only get when you're balls deep in your girlfriend in the middle of the night. I reached over and unlocked the phone.

It opened to the clip of Jennifer in the hot tub. I slid my phone over, so it was right in Lola's eye line as she turned around to see what I was doing. She gasped as she caught sight of the clip.

"What?? Is that-?"

I wordlessly continued slamming my cock into her pussy. Lola moaned loudly and her legs began to tremble. She kept her eyes fixed on the screen as I filled her hole with my cum.

I was lying flat on my back by the time the room had stopped spinning. I realized my phone had been buzzing at irregular intervals for quite a while.

I opened my eyes to find Lola sitting next to me on the bed, staring right at me. When she saw me open my eyes, she smiled and picked up my phone, "so, something you want to tell me?"